The Musicians of Bremen

illustrated by Barbara Vagnozzi

Child's Play (International) Ltd
Ashworth Rd, Bridgemead, Swindon, SN5 7YD UK
Swindon   Auburn ME   Sydney
© 2007 Child's Play (International) Ltd   Printed in Heshan, China
ISBN 978-1-84643-115-9   L150714FUFT09141159
1 3 5 7 9 10 8 6 4 2
www.childs-play.com

D0336199

There was once an old donkey,
who had worked hard
for many years.
"You're not strong enough
any more," said his master.
"I'll have to sell you."

But the donkey did not want to be sold,
and set off for the nearest town of Bremen.
"I've had enough of carrying things
for other people," he thought.
"I think I'd like to be a town musician now!"

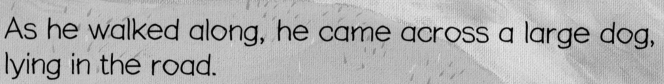

As he walked along, he came across a large dog, lying in the road.

"What's the matter?" he asked. "Are you ill?"

"I'm too old to hunt any more," replied the hound. "My master doesn't want me. I don't know how I will earn my bread now."

"Come with me to Bremen!" suggested the donkey. "I can beat the drum, and you can play the horn!"

They had not walked
much further, when they found a cat in their way.

"I'm too slow to catch mice now," said the cat.
"I'd rather sit by the fire. My mistress was going
to drown me, so I ran away. What shall I do?"

"Well, we need a fiddler," the donkey said.
"Come with us to Bremen!"

As they passed a farmyard,
a large rooster was crowing loudly.

"I am crowing while I can," he explained.
"I am going to be cooked tomorrow."

"Nonsense!" said the three.
"You're coming with us to Bremen.
We need a good singer!"

That night, the animals settled down
to sleep in a wood.

"I'm cold," complained the dog.
"And the ground is hard.   I miss my blanket!"

"There's a light in that window," said the rooster.
"Let's see if we can stay there."

The animals crept up to the window,
and peered in. There at the table
sat a band of fearsome robbers,
who had terrified the villagers
for many months.

"Let's see off those villains!"
suggested the cat.
"Everyone will be very grateful."

"They look stronger than we are," said the donkey.

The animals listened carefully.
Then the dog jumped on the donkey's back,
and the cat stood on top of the dog.
Lastly, the rooster flew up onto the cat.

As they opened the door, the light blew out,
so that the robbers could not see clearly.
The donkey banged on the drum, the dog
played his trumpet, the cat played the fiddle,
and the rooster screeched at the top of his voice.

The robbers looked up and thought
that a monster had arrived! They ran
as fast as they could, out into the dark forest.

Coming home from a party in the village, the owners of the house saw the robbers fleeing. They were so grateful to the musicians that they promised them food and lodging for as long as they wished.

The donkey found a space to sleep in the hay.

The rooster perched on a beam.

The cat stretched out
in front of the fire.

And the dog laid down behind the door.

Out in the cold woods, the robbers
saw that the light had gone out.
"Let's be brave!" said their leader. "I'll go back
to the house and find out what frightened us!"

Creeping into the kitchen, he saw the glistening eyes
of the cat and went nearer. But the cat jumped
at his face, spitting and scratching. The robber ran
to the door, but the dog jumped up and bit his leg.
As he ran across the yard, the donkey gave him
a kick, and the rooster screeched with all his might.

The robber found his way back to his men,
who had heard the terrible commotion
from their hiding place.
"It's no good," he said. "We can't go back there.
There's a terrible creature in the house,
who scratched me with its claws!
Then it took a bite out of my leg,
and kicked me with its very hard hooves!
Finally, it screeched so loudly
I had to run away."

"They look stronger than we are," said the donkey.

"That settles it!" they all said. "Let's get out of here!"
And they ran as far as they could before it was light.

The animals, meanwhile, liked living in the house
so much that they decided to stay awhile.

"I like it here," said the donkey.
"Let's make some music.
We can always go to Bremen tomorrow!"